Dear Priscilla-

With my view of the Boston skyline, I've just had the privilege of reading Albert, The Story of a Lost Dog. What a touching, beautifully wrought story of the love between humans and animals, told in such compelling language and without a shred of sentimentality or skewed point of view. I love the story, and admire you for writing and editing it.

Thank you so much for allowing me to share this fine piece of writing. You inspire me to get to work on the draft I've brought with me of my fourth Nell Prentice novel, titled The Flight of Time, from one of Horace's odes.

Susan Connelly, novel writer [later deceased].

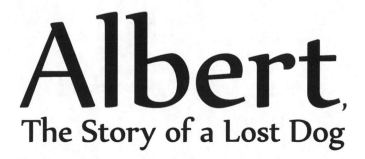

Albert,
The Story of a Lost Dog

Author
Priscilla Q. Weld

ARCHWAY
PUBLISHING

Archway Publishing books may be ordered through booksellers or by contacting:

Archway Publishing
1663 Liberty Drive
Bloomington, IN 47403
www.archwaypublishing.com
1 (888) 242-5904

Because of the dynamic nature of the Internet, any web addresses or links contained in this book may have changed since publication and may no longer be valid. The views expressed in this work are solely those of the author and do not necessarily reflect the views of the publisher, and the publisher hereby disclaims any responsibility for them.

Any people depicted in stock imagery provided by Thinkstock are models, and such images are being used for illustrative purposes only. Certain stock imagery © Thinkstock.

Author photo: Karen Quincy Loberg
Illustrator front cover: Sonny Heston

ISBN: 978-1-4808-2389-1 (sc)
ISBN: 978-1-4808-2390-7 (e)

Library of Congress Control Number: 2015918010

Print information available on the last page.

Archway Publishing rev. date: 04/06/2016

To my two daughters Ingrid Ames Loberg and Karen Quincy Loberg, my inspiration for the daughters in *Albert, The Story of a Lost Dog.*

To my stepsons Thomas Livermore Weld II and John Sargent Weld, for family loyalty and kindness to animals.

To Dr. John Andrew Horton, MD, for his interest in my creative writing and his continuing encouragement.

To the enthusiasm and patience of friends who've waited for *Albert.*

Chapter 1

Albert Thrown from a Truck and Abandoned

The man and dog stood still and took each other's measure, both too close to death to hide their feelings. Using his cane on the cabin porch, the man stepped closer and frowned at the sight before him. A sway and droop in the canine body and the furrowed rib cage mirrored his own slow starvation. He gazed at the dog's black coat, stretched taut across a network of twig-sharp facial bones. The barking dropped to a growl, and soon there was silence. Looking deeper into the brown eyes, the man caught a glimpse of yearning loneliness. "We already have a dog," he murmured.

• • •

In the California Cascade Mountain ranges, an unskilled traveler can quickly find himself in trouble. Streams that rush at flood-speed in springtime and drown those caught in their path will often run dry in a summer drought. Animals and birds of all sizes roam in desperate search for food and water, ready to kill.

Lightning strikes a tree, toppling it slowly until it picks up speed and crashes to earth. Forests of pine and oak sprout close to redwoods. Behind them all, the peaks of stony mountains reach high enough to scrape the clouds. The ground is rough, and the ragged growth of underbrush slows or blocks the way. Tangled huckleberry and sumac cling to stands of cedar. Beauty and danger go hand in hand. A wayfarer passes a grove he thought he left behind an hour before, and must face the growing fear that he is lost. Winter strikes early in the upper ranges.

It was into this wilderness that Albert strayed. He was not a dog who gave up easily. Thrown from a moving truck and abandoned, he kept searching for food and water as well as help from human beings. Mosquitoes and gnats pestered his ears. He shook his head to flap them away and lolled out his tongue to cool off. Hunger jabbed at his stomach, and he dreamed of mounds of kibble. Each night he curled up anywhere, turning his body 'round and 'round in the underbrush or spiky grass.

Despite his misery, he became aware of others in this wild country. Several times there was a flash of color and a wing-beat followed by the scream of captured prey. Sharp-shinned hawks glided, pouncing in midair on smaller birds. A gray eagle gained altitude with a squirrel dangling in its clutches. Winged hunters scanned the area from a height, picking up the slightest motion below and causing small animals to race for safety before it was too late.

Green-black beetles crawled over logs and mountain wildflowers. Other creatures came out only at night while Albert dozed, dimly lit by an early moon. A spotted owl hooted like a barking dog. Raccoons with dark-ringed eyes scrambled downward from their daytime refuge in trees, their claws scratching bark as they descended.

This morning an animal bumbled through the thicket, holding something in its mouth. Albert had never seen a bear cub before. This one looked confused and quite small. It would be easy to snatch its food. He began to follow it, but suddenly his way was blocked with snorting and an overpowering stench. Raising his head, he looked into the angry eyes that glared above the pointed snout of a large bear.

Albert burst into a volley of barks and rushed at it. Rearing on its hind legs, the animal swatted with a paw. Sharp claws grazed Albert's back, and he felt the power behind the wallop. There was no time for false courage. He backed away, but the moving body was almost on top of him. Growls turned into a bellow. Albert knew he could not outrun this enemy. He would have to go down fighting.

A sudden grunt sounded nearby. Romping up to its mother, the cub released its hold on a struggling baby rabbit. Despite a badly bitten body, the rabbit scrambled quickly to freedom. Dismayed at its loss, the cub stood still and wailed while the mother swung away from Albert and carefully sniffed her offspring.

Albert saw his chance. Using the moment to confuse them by jumping into his Frisbee leap, including a special midair twist before he landed, he then turned and rushed from the scene at top speed.

With a final warning snarl, his enemy loped back into the woods, the cub following close behind.

That night, a black and white prowler awakened Albert. He roused himself to investigate, but then his nose began to work. He did not want to get involved with a skunk. He had done that once before at the farm. The animal had squirted him in the face with a liquid that stung his eyes and left a peculiar odor on his fur, no worse to him than many others. Albert did not understand why he was kicked, scolded, and dragged off by the farmer's wife and doused in red juice several times. It was his eyes that hurt.

The sun was high in the sky, and a breeze stirred the treetops. A tantalizing aroma filled Albert's nostrils. Following the scent of meat, he came across a shingled house on a rise. Two men and a woman were gathered around a table under the trees. Moisture collected on Albert's lips and ran over the edges. He trotted up with a hopeful yip.

"Watch out!" the woman screamed, jumping to her feet. "He's foaming at the mouth! He's got rabies!" The men grabbed up pieces of wood and stones and hurled them at Albert.

He yelped when a pebble stung him near his eye as he raced back into the woods. When he was sure they were no longer after him, he sat down, licked his paw, and pulled it across the smarting cut.

His thirst was growing, and that was even worse than hunger. The inside of his mouth felt dry and hot. His skin was an agony of itching, irritated constantly by insects, brambles and barbed grasses. They pricked his mouth and raked his flesh when he moved. Bending his right back leg to scratch the places he could reach with his toenails, he found that scratching made them worse. Fluffs of his own fur flew out and stuck to the bushes around him. Liquid blisters broke and spread on his skin, which puffed up all over again.

Albert was beginning to understand there was little friendliness in the world for a homeless dog. Everyone seemed to be angry or afraid of him. He had to learn to fight for everything he needed. He must find water. The dew that collected on leaves each night barely wet his tongue. Putting his nose to the ground, he began to run in circles, wider and wider. Finally he skidded to a stop, panting and exhausted.

Like tiny bells, a distant tinkling sounded in his ears. He listened for a moment and raised his nose. A fresh aroma filled his nostrils. He pushed himself into a run again, out of the woods and into a clearing.

At first all he could see ahead of him was sea fog spilling over a mountain pass, gathering in the meadow that lay before him. But the tinkling grew louder. With a bark of joy, he rushed straight down the incline. There before him, a stream of water flowed over a stony trench.

Wading in, he slurped it up in great gulps and then lay down and rolled, wetting his fur until it clung in strands to his skinny frame. A minnow scuttled past his nose. He snapped at it, but it swam too fast. Upstream he saw the bear and cub, bent over the brook to drink. Not far from them, a doe raised its head. Seeing several others there, the doe resumed its own drinking.

Albert drank his fill, climbed out, and rubbed his back on a pile of bay leaves. He was relieved to feel the itching subside a little, as the peppermint fragrance of bay drove a few insects from their hiding places in his skimpy coat of fur.

Later, he was taking another drink when he heard a persistent "cobble-obble-gobble!" and caught an odor that was strong and seemed familiar. Albert could not place it. Edging back into the woods, he scrambled downwind to a small clearing and could hardly believe what he saw.

Perched on a tree limb was a row of ungainly birds with fan-like tails and plumage that fluffed out their breasts like the turkeys back on the farm. "Cobble-obble-gobble!" they clucked, and craned their necks to watch the scene below them.

A gray fox was doing the most outlandish things Albert had ever seen. Reclining on its back, the fox stretched one paw into the air and waved gaily at the watchers, then rolled its body sideways like a hoop. With a grin that showed a row of teeth, the animal propelled itself in a whirling dance, spinning around in circles.

The wild turkeys' heads rotated as they watched. In a graceful flip, the fox turned a somersault and grinned again. Standing on both front legs, it crossed the clearing and repeated the acts with variations. Every so often, the birds leaned forward with widened eyes and dangling wattles, then recovered their balance with a start. In a trance, they were unaware of danger.

One of the larger birds slid an inch forward, lost its footing and suddenly tumbled, flailing in the air as it plummeted to earth. With a quick jump, the fox grabbed the helpless bird, pinning down the frightened wing-flap in its jaws, and rushed the prey from the scene. With startled squawks, the other turkeys soon settled back as they had been before. Albert could see they weren't very smart, and he seized his chance. Arranging his face in a foolish grin, he strolled into the clearing.

"Cobble-obble-gobble!" they cried, eying the newcomer.

"Ruffle!" he snuffed, trying to sound like one of them. They simply stared. Perhaps if he roosted as they did, they would mistake him for one of their own. He climbed onto a rock, sat down and wagged his tail, sweeping up a flurry of dry leaves. The turkeys shook out their feathers and ignored him.

Roosting was no good. Rolling sideways looked awkward; so did the dance. He would have to try the somersault, just a neat and simple forward body roll that ended in a winning smile.

Albert crouched and tucked his head between his front legs. Then over he went, slamming his head on the rock as he landed on his back with all four legs extended in the air. "Yawrk!" he yelped, stumbling to his feet.

"Cobble!" they answered. "Cobble-obble-gobble!"

Were they laughing at him? He shook his head to get rid of daylight stars that flickered before his eyes. He would have to think of something easier. If he couldn't turn a somersault, he'd better not try rolling like a hoop, walking on two feet, or even gaily waving. He'd use his Frisbee leap with its midair twist again.

"Ruffle!" he repeated, to put the birds at ease. Leaning way back, he sprang upward in the leap. Twisting on the way back down, he muted his barking. The flap of beating wings and many "wreaks!" sounded in his ears, and he could almost taste his dinner. Several birds must have lost their balance and fallen by now.

Albert hit the ground and opened his jaws, but no turkey flopped into them. Dumbfounded, he looked around and up at the branch, and saw that it was empty. A single feather floated to earth. Way off in the forest, a "gobble!" echoed.

Albert had not foreseen that a jumping black dog that thrashed the sky with a twist and a bark would frighten all the turkeys into permanent departure. He sank onto his haunches, panting and chagrined.

Time passed. Albert found and followed another stream a little farther. Finally, as he leaned over to drink, tramping footsteps reached his ears. Several people came into view. Head cocked, he listened carefully and trailed them at a distance, stopping every few feet for a cautious sniff at the air. Reaching a house set back from the wooded area, a man turned and saw him.

"Go home!" he ordered, and slammed the door shut.

Later, when a curtain parted and a face appeared at the window, Albert pleaded with a soft little moan. The curtain dropped. Patiently he waited, uttering a yip from time to time. The door opened and two bowls were set down outside. "That ought to keep him quiet," a voice said. Albert ran to sniff the bowls, finding kibble in one and water in the other. In no time, he emptied both. All day he waited, but no bowls reappeared.

The mountain air was cold. Twisted shapes of tree trunks and their spreading branches towered over Albert. He had reached another cabin. Shivering in front, he became aware of nighttime people's sounds and scents. He could hear them stirring inside, and he tried several short barks. The door opened.

"Go home," a voice resounded in the moonlit hollow. Albert crawled into the dirt below the porch and dozed with one ear at attention.

For several mornings, when the people appeared he wagged his tail, but they ignored him and drove away. Each evening, the two returned, fed him, and closed the door. This pattern continued long enough to give Albert hope and trust.

But eventually they slammed the cabin door shut, locked it, and carried a few boxy things to the back of their car. The engine coughed and the auto began to roll, gathering speed until it disappeared. Albert settled under the porch to wait.

In the evening, a wood mouse ventured from its hole. He caught it easily but then opened his jaws and released it because he didn't like the taste or the way it scratched and wriggled. Even some bits of sour-tasting garbage he'd found a few days ago at a deserted campfire didn't creep around in his mouth.

Scrambling out from under the porch, he looked around, searching for any sight of the couple or their car. Gusts of wind blew away the smaller sounds. For several days, he hoped and waited. He didn't feel like running anywhere.

At last he understood he had been abandoned again. The farmer and his wife and son who had thrown him from their truck long ago were no more than a dimming memory, along with the day the farmer hit him with a stick and told him how bad he was for "eating a sandwich." Albert had crouched in a corner and cried out in pain while he tried to duck each blow. How could he tell the farmer no one had fed him for the longest time, and the smell of chicken on the outdoor table was too much for him? After that, nobody spoke to him again until they threw him from their moving truck into the wilderness. He didn't remember what they yelled at him when he hit the ground. All he knew was they were laughing.

Despite the treachery he had suffered at human hands, Albert was a people-dog. Without them he felt truly lost.

His ears drooped now and his eyes filled with sorrow, but still, he would guard this place for the ones who had recently fed and deserted him, and hope for their return.

Chapter 2

Albert Confronts Two Strangers at a Cabin

"Okay, we're here, Eric. I'll get the stuff. Don't worry, dear," Ellen said.

"I'm not the worrying kind, Ellen," Eric replied. He fixed a smile on his face, and guiding his descent with a cane, swung his long legs out of the car. "Don't forget my food pump," he added, already knowing she wouldn't.

Approaching the cabin he had designed himself, Eric heard the unmistakable sound of a bark. Frowning, he made his way carefully up the steps that led to the porch, and gazed down into the eyes of a little black dog, its wasted body crouched while it added a growl to warn him away. Gradually the warnings subsided, but Eric sensed the dog's despair. *"We already have a dog," he murmured.*

. . .

Settled inside with Eric, his wife said, "I wonder where that little dog came from. He's half starved. I'll hunt around and see if I can find some dog food. First I'll see if I can calm him down a little."

Eric nodded.

"Meantime you might want to consider a nap, Eric. At least that's what the oncologist recommended."

"I suppose so, Ellen." He picked up his cane and began walking slowly toward the master bedroom, looking around and once more absorbing the flow of the interior layout. There was a combination of sophistication and simplicity there, which Eric knew to be part of his hallmark as an architect. He was thankful he could still turn out his best work.

His basic artistic goal, both inside the home and out, had been to create a home that was a part of the natural beauty of the land itself. With a few trees nearby, the terrain swept along for miles with changes in forestry and altitude as it rose to azure-tinted mountain peaks, bathed in white mist. The cabin itself reflected a spirit of unique serenity.

"Eric, look what I found in the kitchen!" Walking toward him, Ellen waved a bulging bag in her hand. "Kibble! I'm going out now to quiet him a little, feed him on the porch, and then give him a bath in here."

"He's a lucky dog."

She smiled. "You know, dear, I'm glad we came up here again, to see what a fine gift you made to Chris and Mary. They've found a whole new way of life here."

"I wish all the rest of my architectural career had meant so much to me."

Ellen smiled again and then went outside while Eric lay down in the master bedroom.

Through an open window, he heard the bump of full bowls being placed on the porch. Soon came a fast-paced lapping of water, then the distinct sound of crunchy chewing. He closed his eyes, and soon, the light breeze wafting through the trees and the ripples of a brook lulled him to sleep.

"Terminal cancer, stomach and esophagus, inoperable," the city specialist had told Eric abruptly, months ago. "You've got about a year more to go." Mingled with a wave of sadness was Eric's sense of outrage. Never again would he enjoy the exhilaration and peace that lay in hiking through land untarnished by human clutter. His illness and death would affect everything and everyone he loved.

• • •

This morning he had looked closely in the cabin's bathroom mirror. His loss of weight had caused the skin to draw tightly over nearly all his ribs. Aware that Ellen and their two daughters were struggling to accept the finality of the medical verdict, he tried for their sake and his own to make the most of his waning strength and limited independence. He showered, dried himself, and with an effort, pulled on slacks and a shirt.

Ellen had reduced her schedule as a paralegal to have more time with him, and to make sure he received the recommended care. Even with couples like Ellen and himself, who shared a love that grew with the years, trying to deal with new roles as nurse and patient had not been easy.

He knew that as a widow, Ellen would need to deal with her own loss and still provide guidance for Gretchen and Kristin, their two teenage daughters at the threshold of adult womanhood. Though Eric had become increasingly more aware that all three of them had personal strength, he felt he was leaving them at a crucial time in their lives.

• • •

With his career grinding to a halt, Eric had still kept in touch with his friends at the American Institute of Architects. It was there that he heard a story through the grapevine about the rage and discouragement of Chris, whom he had known since high school days in San Francisco.

Chris had saved enough money to buy a small lot at the foot of the mountains. For at least a year, the lot had lain untouched and vacant. Chris finally told Eric proudly that since he had run out of all but a small sum of money, he had consulted a how-to, home construction magazine and decided to execute the architectural plans himself. Later, he admitted that the local planning department had turned down all of his work.

Eric understood what had happened and knew the allure of land ownership in a choice area.

When he and Chris met again, he casually suggested they go up together the following Saturday and take a look. "It's wonderful country. I used to go hiking around there," Eric said.

During their drive from San Francisco, Chris revealed the anger and dismay he had experienced with the planning department. He admitted to Eric that with his incomplete training, he had finally realized his own lack of understanding of the essential elements of architecture and construction. "The guy even had to tell me I'd left out specs in case of fire, in my plans," he said with a wry smile.

Eric nodded. "Pretty damned important, Chris."

"Yeah, I know that now," Chris said. "I even told him I could hook up an arrangement with the brook there on the edge of my land, for extinguishing fire. He let me know in no uncertain terms they got plenty of legal protection against any such use of the brook. Made me feel like a damn fool. He pointed out a fire could destroy not only the cabin but miles of mountain land and real estate that's at a premium."

"Yes, and he's right about the legal protection. There'd be people who'd jump into action to protect the brook. And it's actually useless as a water source, mostly rather shallow water there. Have you thought about consulting a licensed architect? That way, you'd have guidance to other water with a permit and a fee."

Chris shook his head. "Can't afford any of that. Let's go have lunch somewhere, okay?"

"Sure, after we take a look, though."

"Well, all right," Chris agreed. "Seems like I may have to put the land back on the market anyhow. Maybe you could help me figure out about how much I should get for it."

They slowed down and made a turn into more rugged, untamed countryside than that of the evenly tarred streets and copycat housing developments they had passed on their drive from San Francisco. The terrain gradually grew steeper and far less inhabited.

As they pulled onto a level strip of roadside clearing, they caught a glimpse of distant mountain peaks, the sunlight reflecting color against billowing clouds that floated at different heights.

Chris came around to the other side of the car and pointed. "There's a small driveway just ahead of us, really just a leafy gouge in the forest floor." He offered a hand to Eric.

"Thanks, but no thanks. I can actually do this better on my own," Eric explained quietly. With care, he descended from the car, and they moved in single file along a pathway from the roadway to a new scene.

A breeze rippled tiny wavelets through a running brook over at one side. While they stood and took in the tree-lined acreage and the view beyond it, Chris said ruefully, "Well, I guess you can figure out why I fell for it."

Eric immediately knew his own decision. Chris's despair had aroused his sympathy. And for the first time in more than a year, Eric felt the deeply rooted yearning of creation here in an area already dear to him from years of hiking.

He turned to his friend. "It happens I know of a licensed architect who'd be available without a fee, if you decide you'd like to have him."

"I suppose you're kidding," answered Chris.

"Nope," said Eric.

"Well, is he any good?" Chris asked.

Eric smiled. "I believe so."

"What's his name?"

"Oh, it's Eric something or other, some sort of Scandinavian last name."

Chris stared at him in shock. "Eric, you gotta be joking, especially with your—"

"Don't bother to mention my disabilities. I already figured how to deal with them anyway."

"How would Ellen react?"

"I warned her I might try. She thought it'd be great."

. . .

Eric finally convinced his friend that he welcomed the chance to occupy himself in his chosen architectural profession without fee, to design a very special kind of cabin for the mountain lot. He also assured him they had the blessings of both Ellen and Chris's wife, Mary.

Over the following weekend, Ellen and their daughters Gretchen and Kristin worked in San Francisco with Chris, Mary and a neighbor to remove Eric's selection of professional equipment from his home. Carefully, they loaded it into a rental truck for the trip.

Later on and still under Eric's direction, the group set up the load in a roomy old house he had rented near Chris's lot. Eric convinced his friend he needed him and Mary to be there with him until the cabin was completed. She'd be good company for Ellen when the two men were away overseeing construction.

Eric would work first and alone in a quiet wing. He felt strongly that this particular architectural assignment should evolve geographically near the actual building site, to attain his goal for a design that came alive daily as the fruition of a vision. It would respond not only to Chris's dream but to Eric's passionate yearning for a final, uniquely beautiful creation, that enveloped Eric's full attention and drove him onward.

Later, the entire set of documents was approved without a hitch by the planning department.

During construction, Chris and Eric absorbed every detail. Each ear-splitting hammer bang, every tooth-shaking screech of a drill, and even the flying sawdust—all were irresistible to them.

Eric soon saw that the carpentry alone might stretch into winter. Keeping close watch over all the details, he hired some extra help with Chris's okay.

Upon the cabin's completion, Eric stood by himself and gazed. He saw that it reflected a spirit of its own, grown naturally from the land it occupied.

Chris soon joined him. "It's beautiful, Eric, even more than I prayed for. Mary and I hope you'll both come up to the cabin and use it anytime you can. That includes your kids if they want to."

Concerned about his family's feelings, Eric hid as well as he could the steady growth of the cancer that the oncologist confirmed. The San Francisco summer fog rolling into his native city, chilled and depressed him. When he and Ellen visited the cabin, they cherished the daytime warmth and starry skies prevalent in the mountains.

• • •

Sun streamed through the windows and woke them early. Ellen prepared a light breakfast. "Why don't we go outside and eat on the porch?" she asked.

Eric looked at her and grinned. "I think the dog's gone, Ellen. I didn't hear him at all last night."

"Perhaps the meal we fed him made him sleep more soundly," she said hopefully.

"We fed him?"

"All right, you know I did. You didn't want him to go hungry either," Ellen said.

"No, of course not. But please, Ellen, just try to remember all the pets we've had at home—parakeets, cats, turtles, goldfish, a white rat, Gretchen's visiting lamb on a leash, and of course, Kristin's little dog now. The last straw was about three years ago, remember?"

Ellen nodded. "I sure do. The scorpions they caught secretly during our camping trip and hid in a ventilated box at home. Pretty dreadful, I agree. You never did say what you did with them."

"I drove out of town and let them go in their natural habitat, which certainly wasn't hidden in our house in San Francisco."

A scratching and scraping sounded under the cabin porch. Albert crawled out with dried grass stuck to one ear and clumps of earth clinging to his fur. Carefully watching them seated up on the porch, he sat down and offered a couple of eager tail wags.

"You're awfully dirty, pup," Ellen said. "You've been wandering and lost for quite a long time, I think. Come!"

Albert gave her a questioning look, came up the steps, and followed them inside. Eric was surprised to see the dog submit meekly when Ellen stretched out her slender arms and lifted him across the hallway to the bathroom.

Eric decided he'd best stay awhile, in case she ran into any problems with an unknown stray dog.

In the tub, darkened water streamed off his body, revealing every rib, the black color of his fur and some of the oozing sores on his body. With her fingers, Ellen managed to pluck a few of the sharp-pronged foxtail grasses from his shaggy tail and paws. When she tried the same procedure with his legs, the prongs were stuck. Albert didn't make a sound when she finally managed to squeeze and pull only a few of them away from the tangle, though he paid close attention to everything she did.

"He'll need to see a vet for the rest of them," she said to Eric, lifting the dog out and toweling him off. "And he certainly can't go on sleeping under the porch. You saw the filth that poured off his body, not to mention some scars there, as if something or someone had struck him."

"I'm afraid you're right about that."

Over the next few days, Eric patted Albert, but not in the same way Ellen did. Eric called him "dog" and didn't smile as much as Ellen. Walking with his cane, Eric stayed near the cabin most of the time. Ellen left for a little while each day and came back with her light hair damp and a towel wrapped around her swimsuit.

When they went away together, Albert waited anxiously for their return.

One afternoon, Albert was settled down outside, alone with Eric, head resting on his paws. Suddenly there was a crash, and Albert turned to see Eric lying on the porch. The stick he kept in one hand had spun away from him and lay on the ground below. He struggled, trying to stand, but one foot was trapped between posts. Albert ran up and licked his face, but Eric pushed him away.

"That's no good. You're no help."

Albert knew the coolness of that voice, but he had to try again. He came up close and wagged his tail.

"You want to help? Go get my cane." Eric snapped his fingers and pointed at it.

Albert cocked his head and listened, trying to understand.

"Cane, dog, go get it," he ordered. "Go fetch."

The last words, Albert already knew. Jumping off the porch, he grabbed the cane in his teeth, leaped up again, and dropped it close to Eric.

Clasping it in both hands, Eric thrust it firmly onto the porch floor and strained hard to push himself upward. After several tries he managed to reach a sitting position, gripped his leg with both hands, and gave it a tug.

"Ouch!" He grunted as it jerked free. He reached out

and patted Albert, who gave him the biggest smile he could manage.

"That's a pretty smart dog, Ellen," Eric said when he told her later what had happened.

She turned from her packing. "You know we can't leave him here to be alone again. I'll try to find a good home for him, okay?"

"You'd better post signs with our phone number. He could belong to someone around here."

Reluctantly, she nodded.

That afternoon, Ellen and Eric locked up the cabin and started toward their car. Carrying out her husband's feeding equipment, she stored it carefully in the trunk and returned with two suitcases, which she began to lift into the car. Suddenly a black streak raced past her. Before she could stop him, Albert leaped into the driver's seat.

"Oh, doggie, come on, pup. You can't stay there! Get in the back. That's a good boy." She opened the rear door and patted the seat. "Here," she said, but Albert just looked at her, softly moaning and pleading with his eyes. She reached in and gathered him up in her arms. He began to shiver so hard that his teeth clicked together.

"Eric, he's terrified," Ellen said. "He must know what suitcases are, poor dog. He's scared to death we'll leave him here." Carefully she laid Albert on the backseat. The shivering stopped. He licked her hands and wiggled his tail just a little, until he felt almost sure.

They were moving now, and Albert settled his head onto his paws, ready to spring up and resist if anything changed.

Chapter 3

Albert Leaves the Wilderness, Longing to Be the Family Dog

It was dark, and the air was dampened by a San Francisco summer fog. Albert felt the car slow down and turn. He sat up and sniffed at an open space in the window. Lights outlined a house, bigger than the cabin they had just left and blanketed with mist. Other houses nearby looked different. Albert recognized a few of the animal and bird whiffs in the air.

"C'mon, pup. We're home." Ellen opened the car door, looped a spare lead around his neck and lifted him down. He stayed close to her. The air around him was different, damp and cool. Now he recognized the scent of individual birds and several kinds of animals.

A door of the house opened and a young person with long hair stood there staring. Her brown eyes widened.

"Hi, Gretchen, dear," Ellen said. They all embraced, being careful not to get in the way of Eric's cane.

"Where'd you get the dog?" Gretchen asked her mother.

"Well, we didn't really get him. He's apparently lost, and of course we couldn't leave him alone in the mountains. He's starving—you can see his ribs. We'll have to find a good home for him."

"Uh-huh. Is that what Daddy says too?" Gretchen asked.

"Oh, yes, of course," Ellen replied.

"That's for sure, Gretch," Eric said. "First thing tomorrow, your mother will start making calls."

"Hmm. Supposing no one decides to adopt him? How about all those rules—no more pets? I guess they don't apply to you and Mom."

"We're kind of like his foster home till we find a real one," Ellen told her.

Gretchen nodded. "I see." Reaching down, she patted Albert. He raised his head and sniffed her hands, where he caught the definite odor of cats. Another person who looked something like her—except for eyes like Eric's—appeared behind her.

"Hello, Kristin, dear," Ellen said. They all hugged again.

"You got a new dog, Mommy. How come?" asked Kristin.

Ellen repeated her explanation. "We're like his foster parents for now."

"Oh sure, Mommy. He'll be happy here, but he'd better be nice to Poopsie," Kristin said. She snapped her fingers, and a little reddish dog ran up and smelled the new one carefully in the manner of dogs who meet for the first time.

Albert let out a growl that developed into broken barks as he swung around. Clearly he was ready for a fight.

"Knock it off, dog!" Kristin ordered.

"Quiet down, pup," Ellen told him calmly. He caught her tone and subsided.

"Let's hope he behaves himself while he's here," Eric said. "We don't need any fights, and he'd better leave the cat alone too."

"He sure better, Daddy," Kristin agreed, "for his own good. There's no way Rusty's afraid of dogs."

Albert quickly learned a lot in San Francisco. He had to walk on a leash and not pull ahead. He was taught to stay, heel, sit, and obey other orders. He tried hard to please the family and do well with his training so they'd want him to belong to them. Breakfast and supper came every day, with plenty of water to go with them. He slept on a soft bed in his own small room off the porch of his new house.

When they let him out in the fenced backyard, he used his Frisbee jump to tell them when he wanted to come back in. Every time he leaped, the glass top of the half-paned dining room door showed him the family eating at the table. And when they laughed, he wasn't sure why, but he would jump once again until the door was soon opened for him.

Albert carefully slipped from room to room each day. He had learned quickly how to bound up a flight of stairs, something new in his life. The house was very different from anything he had experienced before. The living room was big, with a large and comfortable carpet he liked to lie on. He could see trees out the windows here too, though they looked smaller. He knew one bedroom upstairs was for Gretchen and the other for Kristin. Each room also had the scent of the other dog, Poopsie, and Rusty the cat. The last room he visited was for Eric and Ellen. Here he recognized the scent of the people he was learning to love, especially Eric.

He knew he shouldn't bother Poopsie. She was the only other dog and the oldest of the animals. When he was alone with her, Albert took charge and growled or pushed to show her he was top dog now. Poopsie simply turned her back, sighed, and left the room to be with family.

All Rusty seemed to do was purr, eat, and curl up for naps on Kristin's bed. Albert would have to let him know who was running things. One morning he spotted the cat alone, trotting across the lawn. With a happy bark, he chased after him. The cat turned, fled, and headed for a tree, but Albert sprinted up fast behind. In just a moment, he'd be close enough to catch the yellow tail and pounce. He'd roll him over, do some barking, and maybe give him a little nip to scare him .

Suddenly the cat skidded to a stop, arched his back high so the fur stood up, and began a low yowl and some spitting that sounded like "ff-thhh." Scary yellow eyes glared into

Albert's. Was this the same dumb little cat, the harmless bundle of purring? For a second Albert hesitated, glimpsing a flashback of the huge animal that nearly killed him in the woods.

Pow! A stinging blow whacked him on the ear. The sharp claws dug into his flesh, and quickly the cat swung again. With a yelp, Albert dodged and rolled over on his back to show he was really harmless. Rusty turned disdainfully and trotted away without a backward glance. Albert knew he'd better leave him alone.

Soon after their arrival, Ellen drove Albert to the vet. Lots of barking and a few howls resounded in the small building. He caught a glimpse of several other dogs scratching at their pens. Guiding him through a doorway, Ellen stopped in front of a man in a big coat. She called him "Dr. Berret."

He lifted Albert onto a table and checked him carefully. "I'd say he might be part border collie but mostly spaniel," he told her. "He needs a thorough checkup. We'll do minor surgery today for the festering injuries in his flesh, with medication to aid healing. Soon the usual shots and neutering. A good home where he'll be loved and well cared for—that's the best cure I know of for a full recovery," he added. "I already know you and your family will provide that, if it's your intention to adopt him."

Ellen nodded. "My husband said the last thing all of

us needed was another dog. He won't admit yet that he's warming up to this one."

"Good," said the vet. "Looks like the dog is maybe five or six years old. He needs to gain quite a bit of weight, but in general I think he'll recover nicely. I'd say he found you just about in time."

"He eats well," Ellen said. "He seems to like kibble."

"I'd mix that up with a good brand of canned meat, and provide plenty of drinking water so his insides won't dry out again,'" Dr. Berret advised.

Carrying him into another room, the vet pinched up a fold of flesh and slid a needle into it. Startled, Albert tried to nip at the new intrusion but soon drifted into slumber. When he awoke, he sniffed at his front legs. They were shaven, bandaged, sore, and smelled peculiar, but the sharp burs and grasses that had pierced his skin were gone.

"Poor Albert, you'll feel better soon," Gretchen told him.

The next day Kristin took him on an extra walk, patted him a lot, and kept telling him how good he was. They called him Albert all the time now, because that's what Eric called him.

"Your great-uncle had a dog named Albert," he told his daughters. "I rather liked the name." At least Eric no longer treated him like a stranger. He'd rub him between the shoulders and take him for short walks.

• • •

The stormy night outside grew steadily darker. Torrents of rain pounded on Albert's back. Kristin stood at the kitchen door, calling him to come home. At first, Albert trotted towards her then suddenly stopped. The gate to the yard next door was half open. Curious, he turned around and pushed his way through. The neighbors' car sat in their driveway with the back door open. A new burst of rain beat down, and Albert grabbed his chance for shelter. Jumping inside, he lay down on the floor. If he were quiet, maybe Rick and Nina would let him stay there until the downpour stopped.

Their house door bumped open with its usual squeak, and Rick rushed out through the drizzle. Swearing, he slammed the car door closed, came around, and jumped into the driver's seat.

When the car began to move, Albert decided he'd hop up onto the backseat for a better view. Rick didn't seem to mind. Shafts of their headlights penetrated the rainy darkness, turning it into beams of drizzle as they veered onto the main road. Torrents of water flew off the windshield. Not once did Rick turn around or speak to him. Instead, he leaned forward a little and lifted his hand. Out blasted the kind of noise Albert hated. He drew his ears back and tried to bury his head in the car seat to shut out the wails. He knew Gretchen and Kristin called it rock 'n roll; it sounded like a wolf howling in the mountains.

Something moved outside of the car. Albert turned his head to look. He could barely see through the churning storm a dog about his size, running along beside them. Suddenly it yelped a noisy warning. Rick slammed on the brakes.

"Damn it!" he muttered. "I never knowed Albert follered me. I must've hit him."

He steered the car up onto a shoulder.

Clutching his raincoat close to his body, he climbed out. "Come, Albert!"

He tried to lift the soaked animal from the street. A nasty snarl split the air. The mutt bit at Rick's hand, snarled once more, then raced away into the darkness. Albert himself stood up inside the car and barked loudly.

Reaching into the backseat, Rick touched the friendly nose that greeted him. "It's you, Albert; thank God it's you!"

Albert smiled and wagged his tail.

"You little fool! You been up here in my car all the time. I thought I'd gone and run into you. We're goin' straight back home so your family won't go out huntin' for you."

Albert understood the flood of words and the scared way Rick smelled. He licked him on the chin to reassure him.

Back inside his own house, Albert wondered why Kristin and Gretchen were patting him a lot and laughing. He gave them all a smile anyway, to show how much he loved them.

"Mom, I decided to drive over to Allie Martin's this afternoon," Gretchen said next day. "She and her family just moved here to the city, over by the edge of the big pine grove where the

Jenkins's used to live. My heap has a flat, and Kristin said I could use her MGB for the sightseeing drive I planned for Allie."

Laying her book down on the table beside her living room armchair, Ellen turned to her daughter. "I really don't think you should go over there alone, Gretchen. I've heard they've had trouble."

"Allie's very lonely. The family just moved there to be in a good San Francisco school district for Allie and her little brother. They're new here, and Mimi Brown left Allie out of a big party yesterday. She's got nowhere to go, no car of her own. I told her I'd try to get over there this afternoon and take her sightseeing. I'll be careful, okay?"

"Isn't it a little late in the afternoon for sightseeing?"

"Not really, Mom; it isn't even five yet. Allie misses her old neighborhood. She's very homesick, and being left out of the party didn't help any."

"Well, all right, but please be *very* careful. Lock the car doors and keep most of the windows closed."

"Okay, I'll take Albert with me too. C'mon, boy. We'll go for a ride." She snapped her fingers.

Albert raced to her side, tail wagging. Go for a ride! He'd curl up on the floor mat close to Gretchen in the car. She'd wrap him in her sweater. Maybe they'd go to the beach!

They rolled along past houses and lightly wooded areas. Trees surrounded them on all sides, casting shadows through the filtered shafts of late afternoon sunlight. They coasted along farther until Gretchen stopped the car.

Albert lifted his head a little and sniffed. The air that trickled into the car smelled wrong; he cocked his head, sniffed again, and listened.

The sudden racket of a gunned-up engine sounded close by. A motorcycle swerved around a bend in the small roadway and stopped. Two helmeted men in jeans and jackets jumped off and ran toward them. Albert heard and felt them coming closer. His body stiffened. Before Gretchen could start up the car, one of them clambered up onto the hood. Swinging a hammer, he whacked the windshield. Shards of glass flew inside, barely missing Gretchen and landing on the sweater that covered Albert. He growled, shook his back, and waited for Gretchen's command. But she simply froze. He could sense her fear like his own, facing a bear alone in the woods.

Without a word, the other cyclist strode to the driver's side of the car and tried to open the locked door. Bending down, he picked up a rock and bashed a hole in the window. Ignoring the glass that flew into the car, he reached through the opening and over the jagged window spikes, groping for the door lock.

Gretchen recoiled and fumbled for her wallet. "I have very little money with me," she said, her voice trembling.

A sneer stretched across his wind-toughened face. "*Very little money*," he repeated in a mocking tone. "I seen what ya drivin'," he said, eyeing the new-model car.

Gretchen knew she must fight to keep the door locked as long as she could. She looked down at Albert, crouched, shivering, ready for action. He would help her.

Straightening her shoulders, she spoke more loudly. "Back off or I'll set my dog on you!" The man just laughed.

"Sic 'em, Albert!" Gretchen commanded in a tone Albert knew well. With a sharp bark, he shook the sweater off his back, jumped to her lap, and sank his open jaws into the intruding arm. He felt his teeth penetrate the sleeve and into flesh as he bit down and tasted blood.

The intruder let out a muffled yell and tried to wrench his arm free, but Albert deepened the bite. The rock dropped out of the other hand and onto the ground outside. The helmet fell off, revealing a tangled head of oily hair.

Albert kept his grip tight on the arm with his small but sharp-toothed jaws, holding it down against the jagged points of window glass. Blood oozed from the wounds, staining the sleeve bright red.

The victim's sweating face was contorted with pain and fury. "Come down here off the hood and get me outa this mess, ya stupid moron!" he yelled at his cohort, spitting out a series of four-letter words.

Finally the other man clambered down, reached into the car with his hammer, and tried to strike Albert on the head. Instead the blow landed hard on the dog's nose. With a howl of pain, he released his jaws from the intruding arm.

"You leave that poor dog alone, you damn coward!"

Gretchen shouted. Grabbing the bloodied hammer, she yanked it away from him. It slid from her hand and onto the car floor.

In that brief moment, he found the door's lock, opened it, leaned over and pulled out the other man. As he dragged him over the ground of jagged rocks and thorny undergrowth, he ignored the yelling and cursing. Reaching the roadway, he gripped the injured arm, pulled his companion right up beside the motorcycle and dumped him there. Lifting him into the passenger seat, he strapped him in.

Quickly he stepped forward, swung himself into the motorcycle and gunned it into a speedy roar. The two disappeared as suddenly as they had entered their scene of destruction.

Outside the house a siren wailed once and stopped. Car lights lowered and two uniformed policemen alit, walked up the path, and rang the doorbell. Ellen opened it, Kristin and Gretchen right behind her. Eric soon joined them and introduced himself.

Uniform hats in hand, the two policemen sat. One pulled out a note pad and pen. Albert lay quietly, close to the family, a shield tethered around his neck to keep him from scratching the bandaged wound.

One of the officers, Michael Reilly, introduced himself and Joseph Gilman.

"This is the brave little dog?" asked Reilly.

"Brave is right," Eric said. "He's one in a million, an important part of our family." Albert wagged his tail a little. He loved the sound of Eric's voice and the new way he smiled down at him.

"The suspects already racked up a record of violence, but so far they escaped arrest, " Reilly added. Turning to Gretchen, he said, "We're here to get a full account, miss, and anything you can tell us about 'em will help. Gilman here will be taking notes. This is not a formal deposition. He'll maybe have a couple of quick questions himself. We want you to tell us everything you can remember, all the details. I see your dog got injured."

"Yes. One of those guys busted partway through the window where I was, and stuck his arm inside, trying to find the door lock." Gretchen answered. "Albert—that's our dog—got his teeth right into the arm and pulled it down on the broken glass. He held it there and wouldn't let go till the other guy came down off the hood and whacked the poor little dog with a hammer."

"While we're here, we'd like to snip off a few fur samples of this dog if possible. And later on, miss, you may need to come down and see if you can identify the two at the station. If we're lucky enough to pull 'em in, there's likely be a trial as well."

"I've already cut off some fur, " Eric said. "I happen to be friends with the sergeant who made the appointment for us today, and he asked me to get blood-stained samples soon, so they'd be as fresh as possible. He said they were shorthanded down there, and wanted to move fast on this case. He told me the best way to snip, and to refrigerate them." Eric handed him a small envelope containing blood-stained wisps of Albert's fur. Reilly opened it wider and carefully checked them out.

"They look all right, sir," Reilly told Eric.

Reilly's questioning continued, while Albert watched Gretchen move her hands and talk, and the stranger who kept on scribbling.

Partway into Gretchen's description, Ellen spoke once. "It's lucky our daughter and the dog weren't both killed," she said, her face grave.

Kristin nodded. "They sure messed up the car too, but it's Gretch and Albert that matter now. What a rotten experience!"

"You're right, miss. Wrecking the car first is part of their MO to scare people and prevent any escape," Reilly added. "Then they strip the car and—never mind the rest. I take it from the report that neither man hurt you?" he asked Gretchen.

"That's right."

"You didn't happen to catch the number on the bike's plate?" Gilman asked.

"It wasn't close enough. Sorry." Gretchen looked distressed, and her father moved over and put his arm around her.

"From what you tell us," Reilly commented, "that dog was a godsend and you kept your head. And I take it the dog also tried to fight the man who came down from the hood—and that's how he got his nose injured by the hammer."

"Yes, poor little Albert," Gretchen said.

The questions and answers continued for quite awhile until Reilly motioned his hand at Gilman. They both rose. "I believe we've covered the facts, and thanks," Reilly said. Your testimony should help us. We've already gone over the car for fingerprints, and of course, a check was done for any witnesses, not likely, way out there. Our office also contacted all the hospitals and any docs in the area who might have tended to the one with the injured arm. The story will get picked up by news reporters from the police blotter, and probably run in the papers and TV tomorrow. This is the best lead we got on those two."

He approached Albert, who sat still and eyed him carefully. "What's his name again?"

"Albert," Eric told him, as Reilly leaned over and gave the dog a gentle pat on the head. Albert managed a small tail wag.

"We hope for an early arrest, sir. We'll keep in touch," Reilly told Eric.

"Please do."

Five days later a telephone call came from Michael Reilly. Both suspects had been arrested. Subsequent positive identification by Gretchen, additional evidence gathered on

Albert was soon a favorite among the neighbors, and he endeared himself by escorting many of them to their own front doors. Afterwards he'd go running home so no one would worry about his absence. Albert especially enjoyed Evelyn, who shared a home with her sister two or three houses away. Evelyn always rewarded him with a tasty cookie or two.

Suddenly one day, Albert noticed a large car that made a lot of yowls as it rolled to a stop in front of her house. A kind of back flap swung open while two men jumped out and ran to the front door. It opened quickly for them.

In a short time, they came out again, carrying Evelyn on a sort of bed between them. When they reached the big car, they slid her over the rear flap and inside.

Albert was certain this was wrong. If they were taking Evelyn away, she'd need him to protect her. He'd go quickly, right now. He jumped right in after her when the men weren't looking, and crept until he was close to where she lay.

At that moment, the back flap was pushed and banged closed, and the men ran again to the front. The big car started up with a slight lurch forward. Albert wobbled on his feet and huddled really close to Evelyn. He wanted her to know she had nothing to be afraid of if he stayed near her.

She turned her head and saw him, and the frightened look on her face changed to a tiny smile. She reached out her hand and slid it gently along his back. "We just won't tell anybody right away," she whispered. "Stay right here, Albert. Oooh!" She clapped her hand against her side. Albert knew something hurt. He nuzzled her hand just a few times, and they both settled down.

The big white car coughed and started up again. It seemed to Albert they lurched from side to side, but he just made his paws clutch tighter to the floor mat.

"Atta boy, Albert," Evelyn said and smiled again. "With you around, I'll get well soon." They finally stopped with a jamming of brakes, and the rear flap was opened up again.

"What the hell—where'd that dog come from?" demanded the driver's assistant. "Dogs are strictly forbidden in an ambulance, ma'am."

"This dog is different. He's an important part of our lives, and I certainly don't want him moved away. You understand? I feel ten times better already."

"He can't stay."

"Yes, he can. I don't care what you think or try to say. I pay the bills, and I tell you he stays with me. Just check this out with Dr. Amory. He's your chairman of the board in case you never heard of him—lives a block away from me."

The man started cursing under his breath and slammed the rear flap shut again.

A phone call from Eric to the doctor resulted in visiting

calls for Albert, frequent and accompanied by one of the family. Albert thoroughly enjoyed being led up to Evelyn's hospital room. Her face would break out in smiles. She'd hide her hand under the bed covers, and then before anyone could stop her, slide it out quickly with a cookie saved for him from a recent meal.

Several weeks later, Evelyn was home again and looking well. She let the neighbors know that Albert helped her recover ten times faster than most of the others in the cardiac wing.

Chapter 4

Albert's Love

Time slipped past. For Albert, there was mostly just today, with few memories of his past. He had a family now, and he returned their deep love for him.

Yet still he knew the pangs of worry. This afternoon was walk time again, but his master lay in his bed without moving. Why wouldn't he sit up and take him out? Several times today, Albert saw Ellen quietly crying when she looked at Eric, while he lay with his eyes closed. The girls tried to hide their tears. Albert sensed something was very wrong.

The man in white had just left the house. Every day, he came to Eric's bedside to wash him, fix the bed and feeding tube, and stick something shiny with a sharp point into his arm. The only sounds now were the machine pulsing overhead and Eric's quiet breathing. Albert and Eric were alone together, but Eric didn't stir.

Albert knew he wasn't allowed up on the bed, but perhaps a gentle push wouldn't hurt. He moved a little closer, rose slightly, and nudged. The eyes were open now, and Eric turned his head.

"Sorry, Albert, I can't go out anymore," he said in a low voice. "Too sick, they say." There was a sudden gasp, and Albert sensed his master's pain. He gazed at him. What could he do to help?

His head slowly turned toward Albert once more. "It's all right, I need a little sleep now."

Clearly there'd be no walk today. Albert must stay and guard his master. He settled down and curled up on the rug, still watchful.

That evening the room was darkened. All the family sat close to Eric. His eyes were closed and his breathing came with an effort. Poopsie and Albert lay nearby; Rusty lingered in a corner of the room, hunched under a dressing table with his feline eyes wide open. A light breeze came through the partly open window, stirring the curtains.

"The Hospice nurse is on the way," Ellen murmured. Kristin and Gretchen nodded.

Poopsie suddenly began to run in circles, 'round and 'round, ears back and eyes frantic with fear, toenails scratching as they hit the floor.

Meowing loudly, Rusty raced downstairs and out of sight.

Albert began to shiver. Eric's image was rising slowly

away from his body. He seemed to hover silently, then rise a little more. Albert knew he had to stop him right away. A small leap lifted him up onto the bed and close to Eric, but still he could not stop his beloved master.

Ellen stifled a sob. There was silence in the room until she said, "He's gone."

Her daughters turned and embraced her, weeping with their mother. Albert did not move. His master must return. He would not leave until Eric came back down again.

Later that evening, two funeral attendants were brought upstairs by Ellen. When they entered the room and approached the bed, Albert raised his head and growled a quiet warning.

"Sorry," Ellen said. Moving to the bedside, she lifted Albert into her arms and left the room. Soon the attendants completed their work and carried Eric's body downstairs and out to their vehicle to drive away into the night.

Albert struggled to jump from Ellen's arms and follow them, but she strengthened her hold. "Eric has already gone far away," she told him.

He caught the tearful tone of her voice and rested a little more quietly. Gently she carried him downstairs into the kitchen and lowered him onto his feet.

Gretchen and Kristin tried to coax both dogs to eat their kibble. Poopsie ate only a little and turned away. Albert did not feel hungry at all. He drank some water and walked with quiet determination back up the stairs.

Lying near the closed door, he could not be persuaded to move. Later the daughters leashed both dogs for a short walk, but after relieving himself, Albert pulled until they returned inside the house. Running upstairs, he found the door open. In a moment, he crept inside, leaped onto the empty pillow and lay down his head.

"Mom," Gretchen said, "Kristin and I just don't have the heart to stick Albert in his room off the porch. It's too lonely for him. Okay if we let him stay upstairs in Daddy's room? Poopsie is all right now. She stopped running around in circles and spends a little time with each of us at night. Rusty has settled down too. We both hope pretty soon Albert will understand and give up waiting."

Ellen agreed.

Though he settled into his usual routine with the family, it was clear Albert's spirits were subdued. In the evening after eating very little of the supper offered to him, he went upstairs to Eric's bed and remained there overnight. Every morning and again later on, a member of the family came in to take him out for walks..

• • •

Dr. Berret reported to Gretchen and Kristin the results of Albert' s next checkup. No basic ill health was evident, he said, but added, "Albert is underweight again and does have an irregular heartbeat. I understand your father died. I'm really sorry; it must be hard for all of you. Family pets often sense what's happened, and do their grieving in quite different ways."

Gretchen described to him Albert's nightly vigil. "When Albert first wandered into our lives, my father didn't seem to like him much, but gradually Albert won him over until they became very close. It seems our dog is heartbroken, still mourning my father's death. He keeps waiting for him to come back again and can't understand where or why he's gone."

The veterinarian nodded. "I hope eventually he'll put on some weight and accept his loss. Albert is an unusual dog. He's very lucky he found all of you. I've come to understand quite a lot about the animals that come in here.

"My experience and examinations tell me this loyal, affectionate dog sometime ago received some clearly abusive treatment in the wrong hands. And then came another lengthy ordeal, fighting for his life in the mountains. Since he wandered into your lives, all of you have given him what is probably the best life he's ever had." He looked down again at Albert, who gave him as good a smile as he could manage.

• • •

Albert sighed deeply. Why had his master gone away without him? He knew the family wanted Eric back home too. They stayed together a lot, talking about "Daddy." When they cried, Albert would go over and put a paw in Gretchen's lap or Kristin's, or gently nuzzle Ellen. They would talk to him and each other and smile a little.

Albert felt very tired and sad tonight. He'd go upstairs and sleep. Perhaps when he woke up, Eric would be there waiting for him. He walked quietly into the bedroom and climbed onto the bed. Laying his head on Eric's pillow, he closed his eyes.

A little later, Albert slipped away from them with the highest Frisbee leap of all, to take his place by his master's side.

++++

Author Priscilla Q. Weld was born on Martha's Vineyard Island, MA. She attended Milton Academy with a scholarship and Sarah Lawrence College in Bronxville, NY for her diploma. Later, she attended author/instructor Leonard Bishop's nighttime fiction workshop in Berkeley, CA for three years.

When she was only ten, Priscilla submitted her article to a contest run by St. Nicholas magazine. Contestants were told to write about "The most unusual thing your dog has ever done." Her English setter had climbed a tree to chase a cat, and the article won a first prize.

As a city staff reporter for the New York Herald Tribune, she interviewed Adolf Hitler's nephew in the Bronx. The Nazi dictator's relative had become an American citizen, accepted into the U.S. Army.

Other assignments covered included the arrivals in New York of Eleanor Roosevelt and Golda Meir.

One unusual news subject was a poor horse whose strenuous job was to pull an over-loaded cart in downtown Manhattan. His hind leg got trapped in a manhole, and he had to be lifted out by a specially adapted derrick.

In a few years, Priscilla left Manhattan and moved to the City By The Bay. There she married architect Lee T. Loberg, San Francisco native. They had two daughters, Ingrid and Karen. Priscilla wrote press releases for three creative entities: the California Historical Society, an artistic painter named Jerry Jolley, and a children's theater.

Rapidly growing daughters were a prime consideration in their parents' lives. Her husband opened up a small architectural office downtown, and Priscilla became certified as a California court reporter. As a free-lancer for eleven years, she was well remunerated. She particularly enjoyed maritime reporting, when she climbed on board ships at port and covered attorneys' depositions there. She believes that court reporting is a very good background for creative writing. Accuracy and handling the unexpected are equally important.

When she was widowed, she went back east to assist her Boston family. Subsequently she was married to Lothrop M. Weld, Jr., retired senior VP with a Boston real estate firm. In Duxbury, MA, they lived together with their dogs near the ocean until her husband's death.

Priscilla returned to California and also to her favorite career, creative writing. Two daughters, two stepsons, A-1 friends, relatives and others add sunshine to her life.

####